Zelda and Ivy
THE RUNAWAYS

Laura McGee Kvasnosky

CANDLEWICK PRESS

To Julie and Meg and Margaret
with love and thanks

First paperback edition in this format 2013

The Library of Congress has cataloged the hardcover edition as follows:
Kvasnosky, Laura McGee.
Zelda and Ivy: the runaways / Laura McGee Kvasnosky — 1st ed.
p.   cm.
Summary: In three short stories, two fox sisters run away from home, bury a time capsule, and take advantage of some creative juice.
ISBN 978-0-7636-2689-1 (hardcover)
[1. Foxes—Fiction. 2. Sisters—Fiction.]   I. Title.
PZ7.K975Zen 2006
[Fic]—dc22   2005054282

ISBN 978-0-7636-6635-4 (paperback)

APS 18 17 16 15
10 9 8 7 6

Printed in Humen, Dongguan, China

This book was typeset in Galliard and hand-lettered by the author-illustrator.
The illustrations were done in gouache resist.

Candlewick Press
99 Dover Street
Somerville, Massachusetts 02144

visit us at www.candlewick.com

CONTENTS

Chapter One
THE RUNAWAYS

"Dad's making cucumber sandwiches for lunch," said Ivy.

"Not again!" said Zelda. "That's it. I'm running away."

Zelda stuffed her lucky jewel, PJs, blanket, writer's notebook, and an extra pair of socks into her suitcase.

"I'm coming too," said Ivy.

She packed her Princess Mimi doll, PJs,
tea set, and Go Fish cards.

Zelda marched across the backyard.

Ivy followed.

Zelda spread her blanket behind the
butterfly bush. "Here's a good spot," she
said. "We can see the house, but no one in
the house can see us."

The fox sisters peeked through the bush

at their parents.

"Mom and Dad will really miss us,"

said Ivy.

"Yes," said Zelda. "They'll be sorry they

made us cucumber sandwiches."

"I'm a little hungry,"
said Ivy.

"We can't give in," said
Zelda, "or we'll be
eating cucumber
sandwiches for the rest
of our lives."

Ivy filled her teapot from the garden hose and peeked in the window.

"They don't seem to be missing us," she reported.

"It may take a while," said Zelda. "Lucky you brought your cards."

Zelda and Ivy played fourteen hands
of Go Fish. Still their parents did not come
looking for them.

"I wish we had cookies," said Ivy.

"Be tough," said Zelda. "We may have
to sleep here tonight."

The fox sisters put on their PJs and waited for dark. To pass the time, they decorated the edge of the blanket with pussy-willow puffs.

They figured out their names backwards: Adlez and Yvi.

They wrote a two-chapter book about a worm named Philip.

When they finished, they could hear their parents talking and laughing in the kitchen.

"We should have left a note," said Ivy.

Pretty soon salsa music drifted out the window.

"I bet they're dancing," said Ivy. "I sure love to dance."

"Oh, all right, Ivy," said Zelda. "I don't want you to feel left out. Let's go home."

The fox sisters packed up their stuff and

scurried back across the lawn.

Their dad met them at the kitchen door.

"Oh, there you are!" he said. "We saved you each a delicious cucumber sandwich."

Chapter Two
THE TIME CAPSULE

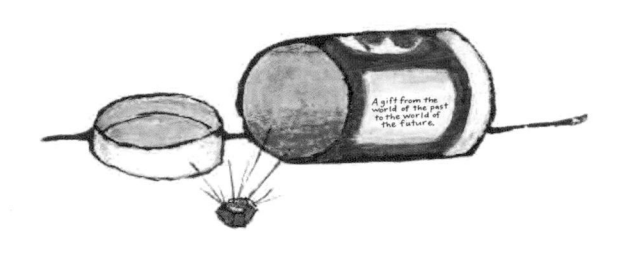

Zelda wrote the label with a fat pen:

**A gift from the
world of the past
to the world of
the future.**

"This is a time capsule," she said.

She rubbed her lucky jewel against her
shirt and dropped it into the box. "A
hundred years from now, someone will
open this box and find my lucky jewel.
What are you going to put in?"

"How about
our worm book?"
said Ivy.

"Come on,"
said Zelda. "Put in
something really
good. Remember,
it's for the children
of the future."

Ivy sighed. She hugged Princess Mimi
and added her to the box.

Zelda buried the time capsule under the
cherry tree.

Later that day, Ivy sat on the swing and

drew circles in the dirt with her paw. "If only

I had Princess Mimi, I could play castle."

Inside the house, Zelda worked on her
piano recital piece. "If only I had my lucky
jewel, I could get that crossover hands part."

Outside, Ivy could stand it no longer. She dug up the time capsule and pulled out her doll. Then she noticed: the box was empty.

Ivy heard a noise in the bushes. She stuffed Mimi back into the box.

The bushes rustled again. Out stepped

Zelda. "What're you doing?"

"Just checking on Princess Mimi," Ivy

admitted. She took a deep breath. "Zelda,

your lucky jewel is missing!"

Zelda narrowed her eyes. "I might have had to borrow it back for my piano recital."

Ivy opened the box again. "I need Princess Mimi back, too."

Zelda nodded. "Let's put in our worm book. Now that I think of it, I'm sure the children of the future would prefer a good story."

Chapter Three
THE SECRET CONCOCTION

Early one morning, Zelda sat down to write

a haiku poem for her grandmother.

Ivy came in, shaking a jar of liquid.

"What's that?" asked Zelda.

"I'm making a secret concoction," said

Ivy. She poured in some orange juice.

"You should add glue," said Zelda.

"I don't think so," said Ivy. She mixed in a mint leaf and an eyelash.

"Put in cinnamon hearts," said Zelda. "Make it a *love* potion."

Ivy screwed the top
back on the jar. "No,"
she said.

"What are you
going to do with it?"
asked Zelda.

"We'll see,"
said Ivy. She gazed
at the jar. She wasn't
sure herself.

Zelda went back to her haiku. She
rubbed her forehead with her lucky jewel.
She cracked her knuckles.

"Rats," she said. "I'm stuck."

"Why not take a break?" asked Ivy.

Ivy opened a bag of Nutty Crunchies
and gave a handful to Zelda. Then she
popped one into the jar.

Zelda sat down again. "I will finish this
poem if it's the last thing I do."

Eugene came over to play Go Fish with Ivy. They were on their eighth game when Zelda jumped up and stomped away.

"I give up," she said.

"Zelda is having a hard day," said Ivy. "She's out of ideas."

"I know what she needs," said Eugene. "Creative juice. Creative juice gets the ideas flowing."

"So what exactly is creative juice?" asked Ivy.

"I'm not sure," said Eugene. "It's a secret concoction."

"Perfect!" said Ivy.

Eugene and Ivy got to work.

When Zelda came back downstairs, Ivy
handed her a present.

"Open it," said Eugene.

Zelda tore off the paper and read the
label. "Creative juice! How does it work?"

Ivy sprinkled the creative juice on Zelda's head. Some of it spilled on the journal as well.

"My poem is ruined!" wailed Zelda. She

threw herself down on the floor.

Then she looked carefully at her journal.

She turned it one way and the other.

"Wait a minute," she said. "This looks like a lake at sunset." She got out her colored pencils. "I'll make a picture for Grandmother instead!"

"Wow," said Eugene. "That creative juice really works."

Ivy smiled. "Lucky I got the recipe right."